NOTE TO THE READER
"Omu" (pronounced AH-moo)
is the Igbo term for "queen."

n the inland
sinterpretatio
expedient so
chools in the
the study re
the study.
locating a s
55

THANK YOU, OMU!

OGE MORA

Ⓛ Ⓑ

LITTLE, BROWN AND COMPANY

NEW YORK BOSTON

ON THE CORNER of First Street and Long Street, on the very top floor, Omu was cooking a thick red stew in a big fat pot for a nice evening meal. She seasoned and stirred it and took a small taste.

"What a delicious stew!" Omu said. "Tonight's dinner will surely be the best I have ever had."

With that, Omu put down her spoon and went to read a book before supper. As the thick red stew simmered on the stove, its scrumptious scent wafted out the window and out the door, down the hall, toward the street, and around the block, until—

KNOCK!

Someone was at the door.

When Omu opened it, she saw...

…a little boy.

"LITTLE BOY!" Omu exclaimed. "What brings you to my home?"

"I was playing with my race car down the hall when I smelled the most *delicious* smell," the little boy replied. "What is it?"

"Thick red stew."

"MMMMM, STEW!" He sighed. "That sure sounds yummy."

Omu thought for a moment. She was saving her stew for dinner, but she *had* made quite a bit. It would not hurt to share. "Would you like some?"

The little boy nodded.

And so Omu spooned out some thick red stew from the big fat pot for her nice evening meal.

"THANK YOU, OMU!" the little boy said, and went on his way.

With that, Omu closed the door and went back to her book.
As she read, her thick red stew's scrumptious scent wafted
out the window and out the door, down the hall,
toward the street, and around the block, until—

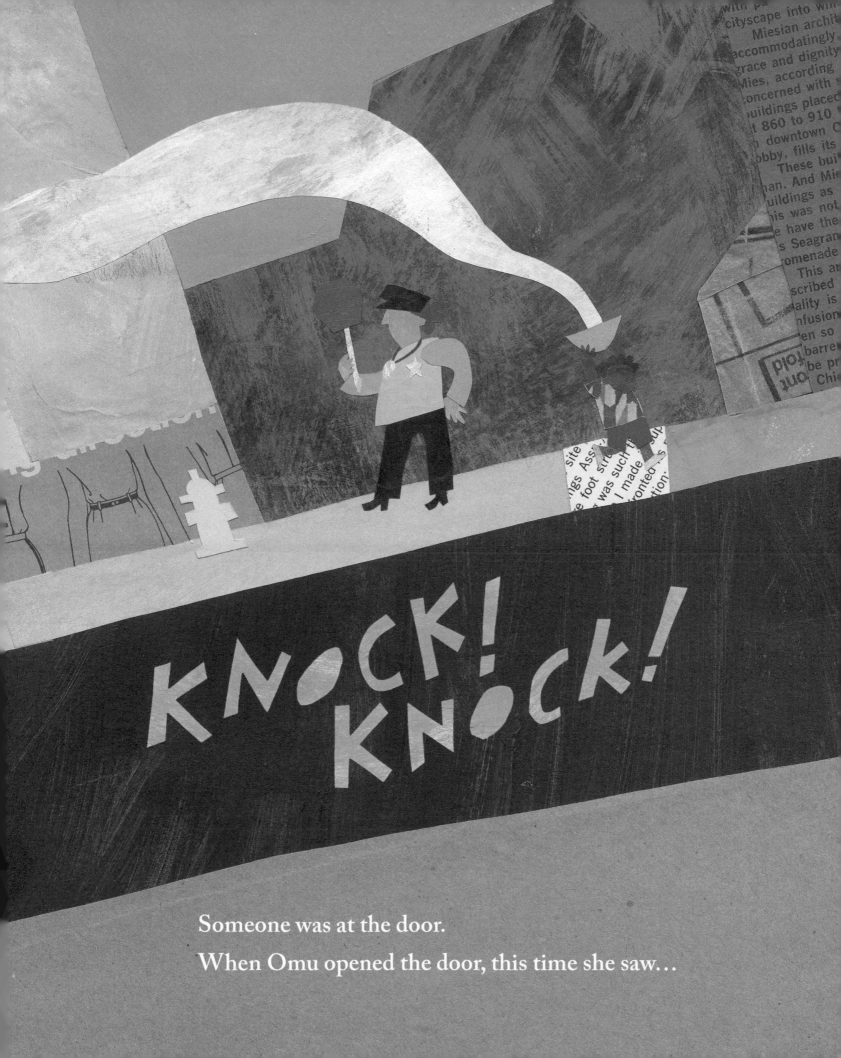

KNOCK!
KNOCK!

Someone was at the door.

When Omu opened the door, this time she saw…

…a police officer.

"MS. POLICE OFFICER!" Omu exclaimed. "What brings you to my home?"

"I was on duty down the street when I smelled the most *delicious* smell," Ms. Police Officer replied. "What is it?"

"Thick red stew."

"AHHHH, STEW!" she said, and her mouth watered. "That sounds mighty tasty."

Omu thought for a moment. There was still enough to share. "Would you like some?"

The police officer nodded.

Once again, Omu spooned out some thick red stew from the big fat pot for her nice evening meal.

"THANK YOU, OMU!" the officer said, and went on her way.

And so for the second time, Omu closed the door and went back to her book. Sure enough, as she read, her thick red stew's scrumptious scent wafted out the window and out the door, down the hall, toward the street, and around the block, until—

KNOCK KNOCK KNOCK KNOCK!

Again, someone was at Omu's door.
This time when she opened it, she saw…

…a hot dog vendor.

"MR. HOT DOG VENDOR!" Omu exclaimed.
"What brings you to my home?"

"I was selling my hot dogs down the block when I smelled
the most *delicious* smell," Mr. Hot Dog Vendor replied.
"What is it?"

"Thick red stew."

"OOOOO, STEW!" The vendor licked his lips.
"That sounds quite delectable."

So Omu spooned out some thick red stew from the big fat pot for her nice evening meal.

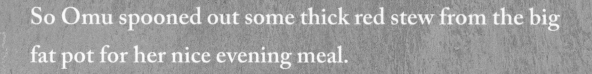**"THANK YOU, OMU!"** the hot dog vendor said, and went on his way.

Throughout the day, people from all across the
neighborhood knocked on Omu's door. She
fed a shop owner, a cab driver, a doctor, an actor,
a lawyer, a dancer, a baker, an artist, a singer,
an athlete, a bus driver, a construction worker....
Even the mayor stopped by!

And each time they knocked, Omu shared.

Soon, the sky darkened, the streetlights brightened, and it was finally time for dinner.

But when Omu opened her big fat pot of thick red stew for her nice evening meal…

...IT WAS EMPTY.

Omu sniffled. "There goes the best dinner I ever had!" Sorry and blue, she sat at the table with her empty pot, until—

KNOCK! KNOCK! KNOCK!

KNOCK!

KNOCK! KNOCK!

KNOCK!

Who could that be? Omu wondered. When she opened her door, she saw…

…the little boy? The police officer? The hot dog vendor? The shop owner, the cab driver, the doctor, the actor, the lawyer, the dancer, the baker…why, everyone she fed today was at her door!

"I'm sorry, everyone!" Omu sighed. "My thick red stew is all gone. I have nothing left to share."

The little boy tugged at Omu's sleeve. "Don't worry, Omu. We are not here to ask…

WE ARE HERE TO GIVE."

The police officer carried in a fresh salad. The mayor entered with a roast chicken. The baker brought a collection of sweet goodies. Even the little boy presented Omu with something special in a shiny red envelope.

Everyone who had knocked on Omu's door that day squeezed inside her tiny apartment, and together they ate, danced, and celebrated. While Omu's big fat pot of thick red stew was empty, her heart was full of happiness and love.

That dinner was the best she had ever had.

AUTHOR'S NOTE

In Igbo, the Nigerian language of my parents, "omu" means "queen." Yet for me, growing up, it meant "Grandma."

When my grandmother cooked, she danced and swayed her hips to the radio as she stirred what was often a large pot of stew. In the evening, my family would come together at the dinner table for her meal. If a neighbor was visiting, they were invited. If a friend had stopped by, they were invited. Everyone in the community had a seat at my grandmother's table.

While my grandmother has since passed away, her giving heart has stayed with me. I see it in my mother, my godmother, my teachers, my mentors, and the other countless powerful women who have shaped my life.

This book is a celebration of their loving, giving spirit.

Thank you!

ABOUT THIS BOOK

The collages for this book were created with acrylic paint, china markers, pastels, patterned paper, and old-book clippings. This book was edited by Andrea Spooner and art directed by Sasha Illingworth with Angela Taldone. The production was supervised by Erika Schwartz, and the production editor was Jen Graham. The text was set in Adobe Caslon Pro, and the display type is PaperCute.